Dear Parents and Educators,

Welcome to Penguin Young Readers! As parents and educators, you know that each child develops at his or her own pace—in terms of speech, critical thinking, and, of course, reading. Penguin Young Readers recognizes this fact. As a result, each Penguin Young Readers book is assigned a traditional easy-to-read level (1–4) as well as a Guided Reading Level (A–P). Both of these systems will help you choose the right book for your child. Please refer to the back of each book for specific leveling information. Penguin Young Readers features esteemed authors and illustrators, stories about favorite characters, fascinating nonfiction, and more!

Good Night, Good Knight

LEVEL 2

GUIDED
READING
LEVEL
I

This book is perfect for a **Progressing Reader** who:
• can figure out unknown words by using picture and context clues;
• can recognize beginning, middle, and ending sounds;
• can make and confirm predictions about what will happen in the text; and
• can distinguish between fiction and nonfiction.

Here are some **activities** you can do during and after reading this book:
• Picture Clues: Use the pictures to tell the story. "Read" the illustrations.
• Make Predictions: What will the little dragons want before going to bed?
• *Night* and *knight* are homophones—words that sound the same, but are spelled differently and mean different things. Can you come up with homophones for the following words from the story?

| heard | know | poor | see | to |

Remember, sharing the love of reading with a child is the best gift you can give!

—Bonnie Bader, EdM, and Katie Carella, EdM
    Penguin Young Readers program

*Penguin Young Readers are leveled by independent reviewers applying the standards developed by Irene Fountas and Gay Su Pinnell in *Matching Books to Readers: Using Leveled Books in Guided Reading*, Heinemann, 1999.

For Nana and Papa John, who know all
about dragons—SMT

For S.U.—JP

Penguin Young Readers
Published by the Penguin Group
Penguin Group (USA) Inc., 375 Hudson Street, New York, New York 10014, USA
Penguin Group (Canada), 90 Eglinton Avenue East, Suite 700, Toronto, Ontario M4P 2Y3, Canada
(a division of Pearson Penguin Canada Inc.)
Penguin Books Ltd., 80 Strand, London WC2R 0RL, England
Penguin Group Ireland, 25 St. Stephen's Green, Dublin 2, Ireland (a division of Penguin Books Ltd.)
Penguin Group (Australia), 250 Camberwell Road, Camberwell, Victoria 3124, Australia
(a division of Pearson Australia Group Pty. Ltd.)
Penguin Books India Pvt. Ltd., 11 Community Centre, Panchsheel Park, New Delhi—110 017, India
Penguin Group (NZ), 67 Apollo Drive, Rosedale, Auckland 0632, New Zealand
(a division of Pearson New Zealand Ltd.)
Penguin Books (South Africa) (Pty.) Ltd., 24 Sturdee Avenue,
Rosebank, Johannesburg 2196, South Africa

Penguin Books Ltd., Registered Offices: 80 Strand, London WC2R 0RL, England

Text copyright © 2000 by Shelley Moore Thomas. Illustrations copyright © 2000 by Jennifer Plecas.
All rights reserved. First published in 2000 by Dutton Children's Books and in 2002 by Puffin Books,
imprints of Penguin Group (USA) Inc. Published in 2011 by Penguin Young Readers, an imprint of
Penguin Group (USA) Inc., 345 Hudson Street, New York, New York 10014. Manufactured in China.

The Library of Congress has cataloged the Dutton edition under
the following Control Number: 99028415

ISBN 978-0-14-230201-9   10 9 8 7 6 5 4 3 2 1

PENGUIN YOUNG READERS

LEVEL
PROGRESSING READER
2

Good Night,
Good Knight

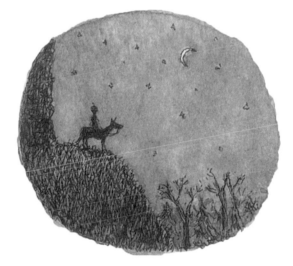

by Shelley Moore Thomas
pictures by Jennifer Plecas

Penguin Young Readers
An Imprint of Penguin Group (USA) Inc.

Once there were
three little dragons.
They lived in a dark cave.
The cave was in a dense forest.
The forest was
in a faraway kingdom.
The poor little dragons
were very lonely in
their deep dark cave.

In the kingdom
there was a Good Knight.
Every night he kept watch.
He watched from
a crumbly tumbly tower.
It was on top
of a very tall wall.

One night the Good Knight
was on his watch.
He heard a very large,
very loud roar.

So the Good Knight

left the crumbly tumbly tower.

He climbed down the very tall wall.

He jumped on his horse.
"Away!" he said.
He galloped through
the king's forest.
Clippety-clop.
Clippety-clop.

He came to the deep dark cave.

Inside he saw the first little dragon.

"What's this?" he asked.

"Methinks it is a dragon!"

And he drew his

shimmery, glimmery sword.

The dragon had on his jammies.

He was all ready for bed.

"Oh good.

You have come,"

said the dragon.

"Could you bring me
a drink of water?
Please.
Then I can go to sleep."

The Good Knight did not know
what to think.
But he was a good knight.
So he got a drink of water.
He gave it to the dragon.

Then he tucked him into bed.

"Good night, good dragon.

Sleep well, sleep tight,"

said the Good Knight.

Then he galloped away.

The Good Knight went back
through the king's forest.
Clippety-clop.
Clippety-clop.

He got off his horse.
Thud.
He climbed up the very tall wall
to the crumbly tumbly tower.
There he stood on watch.

He stood on watch
for five minutes.
Then he heard another
very large,
very loud roar.

"I don't believe this,"

he said.

He left the crumbly tumbly tower.

He climbed down

the very tall wall.

He jumped on his horse.

"Away!" he cried.

He galloped through

the king's forest.

Clippety-clop.

Clippety-clop.

He came to the deep dark cave.

The second dragon was
in her jammies.
She was all ready for bed.
"Oh good.
You have come,"
said the second dragon.
"Could you read me a story?
Please.
Then I can go to sleep."

"And could I have
another drink of water?"
said the first dragon.

The Good Knight did not know
what to think.
But he was a good knight.

So he read the dragon a story.

Then he tucked her into bed.

He got the first dragon
another drink of water.
Then he tucked him into bed.

"Good night, good dragons.
Sleep well, sleep tight,"
said the Good Knight.
Then he galloped away.

The Good Knight went back
through the king's forest.
Clippety-clop.
Clippety-clop.

He got off his horse.
Thud.
He climbed up the very tall wall
to the crumbly tumbly tower.
There he stood on watch.

He stood on watch
for two minutes.
Then he heard another
very large,
very loud roar.

"This is too much,"

he said.

He left the crumbly tumbly tower.

He climbed down the very tall wall.

He jumped on his horse.

"Away!" he cried.

He galloped through

the king's forest.

Clippety-clop.

Clippety-clop.

He came to the deep dark cave.

The third dragon had

on his jammies.

He was all ready for bed.

"Oh good.
You have come,"
said the third dragon.
"Could you sing me a song?
Please.
Then I can go to sleep."

"And could you read me
another story?"
said the second dragon.

"And could you get me
another drink of water?"
said the first dragon.

The Good Knight did not know
what to think.
But he was a good knight.
So he sang the dragon a song.
Then he tucked him into bed.

He read the second dragon
another story.
Then he tucked her into bed.

He got the first dragon
another drink of water.
Then he tucked him into bed.

"Good night, good dragons.
Sleep well, sleep tight,"
said the Good Knight.
Then he galloped away.

The Good Knight went back
through the king's forest.
Clippety-clop.
Clippety-clop.

He got off his horse.
Thud.
He climbed up the very tall wall
to the crumbly tumbly tower.
There he stood on watch.

He stood on watch
for one minute.
Then he heard
the largest,
loudest roar of all.
"Not again," he said.

He left the crumbly tumbly tower.

He climbed down the very tall wall.

He jumped on his horse.

"Away!" he cried.

He galloped through
the king's forest.

Clippety-clop.
Clippety-clop.

He came to the deep dark cave.
"Oh good.
You have come,"
said all three dragons.

"Let me guess,"
said the Good Knight.
"Another drink of water?"
"No," said the first dragon.

"Another story?"

"No," said the second dragon.

"Another song?"

"No," said the third dragon.

"Then WHAT DO YOU WANT?"
cried the Good Knight.

"We need a good-night kiss,"
said the little dragons.
And they lifted
their scaly little cheeks.

"This is going too far,"
said the Good Knight.

But he was a good knight.
So he bent and kissed
each scaly little cheek.
"Good night, good dragons.
Sleep well, sleep tight,"
he said.
The dragons said,
"Good night, Good Knight."

The Good Knight left the cave.

He waited outside.

He heard the loud dragon snores.

Then the Good Knight went home
through the king's forest.

Clippety-clop.

Clippety-clop.

He got off his horse.

Thud.

"Now," said the Good Knight,
"maybe I can get a
good night's sleep."

And that is just
what he did.
Sleep well, sleep tight,
Good Knight.